MY BROTHER IS A
SUPERHERO

Also by Dyan Sheldon

MY BROTHER IS A VISITOR FROM ANOTHER PLANET

DYAN SHELDON

MY BROTHER IS A SUPERHERO

Illustrated by
Derek Brazell

VIKING

For Tom and Dan

VIKING

Published by the Penguin Group
Penguin Books Ltd, 27 Wrights Lane, London w8 5tz, England
Penguin Books USA Inc., 375 Hudson Street, New York, New York 10014, USA
Penguin Books Australia Ltd, Ringwood, Victoria, Australia
Penguin Books Canada Ltd, 10 Alcorn Avenue, Toronto, Ontario, Canada m4v 3b2
Penguin Books (NZ) Ltd, 182–190 Wairau Road, Auckland 10, New Zealand

Penguin Books Ltd, Registered Offices: Harmondsworth, Middlesex, England

First published 1994
10 9 8 7 6 5 4 3 2 1

Text copyright © Dyan Sheldon, 1994
Illustrations copyright © Derek Brazell, 1994

The moral right of the author has been asserted

Filmset by Datix International Limited, Bungay, Suffolk
Printed in England by Clays Ltd, St Ives plc
Set in 14/17 pt Monophoto Baskerville

A CIP catalogue record for this book is available from the British Library

ISBN 0–670–85132–9

Chapter One

*T*he score was two-all and the crowd was on its feet. There was less than a minute to play.

Babidge got the ball from Anuli. Anuli passed it to King. King, cornered, spun round and kicked fiercely. It was a desperate move, but a lucky one. The ball sailed clear across the field to where Andrews stood waiting – all alone. The crowd went mad. Andrews raced towards the goal like a lizard. A lizard with really good foot co-ordination.

'An-*drews*! An-*drews*! An-*drews*! An-*drews*!'

Faster and faster. Time ticked away.

The crowd was beside itself with tension and excitement.

'An-*drews*! An-*drews*! An-*drews*! An-*drews*!'

And then Cross and Bui came out of nowhere. Foaming at the mouth, Cross closed in from the right. Bui bore down from the left in a mist of mud, his eyes wild.

'An-*drews*! An-*drews*! An-*drews*!'

Andrews looked around in panic. He was feet from the goal, but he was stranded between Cross and Bui and Hogan, the goalie. He didn't have a hope, and he knew it.

The commentator was counting the seconds. 10 . . . 9 . . . 8 . . .

A ripple ran through the stadium. It was a miracle! Another player had appeared behind Bui.

The crowd changed its chant. 'Wig-*gins*! Wig-*gins*! Wig-*gins*!' it roared.

I'd been waiting all season for this chance. The chance to be a hero. The chance to score the winning goal. Like a bullet in a striped jersey and muddy boots, I streaked past Bui, cutting between him and Andrews. My blood thundered. My heart raced. My training and patience were about to pay off. My moment had come at last! There was the goal post. There was the goalie. There was the opening. I aimed my kick.

5 . . . 4 . . . 3 . . .

But before my foot could touch the ball I lost my balance and came down on my back. Helpless, I lay there watching as the ball soared over me – and straight into the goal.

Time!

The stadium went wild. Even the benches seemed to be screaming. Laughing and shouting, the team lifted the scoring player on their shoulders.

The crowd was still chanting. 'WigginsWigginsWigginsWiggins!'

Someone stepped on my leg as they carried my brother off the field.

I was practically crying when I woke up. How come? I wondered. How come even in my sleep my brother always beat me? I could understand if it was Keith's dream. That would make sense. Of course he'd be sure he was the hero in his own dumb dream. He thinks he's smart, my brother. He's always trying to make me look stupid, and most of the time he succeeds. But this was *my* dream. It was my dream, and I still lost out to Keith. I might as well have been awake. It didn't seem fair.

I opened my eyes slowly. Elvis, my dog, was stretched out across my legs, sound asleep, and on the other side of the room Keith was still snoring. My brother is the only person I know who sleeps flat on his back with his hands under his head. Most of the time I don't notice any more, but this morning it really bothered me. I looked over at him. I'm sort of an average size for my age, but my brother's big. He's not only tall, he has all these muscles from doing so many sports. He was lying there as if he was watching a film on the ceiling. He had a big smile on his face. With my luck, Keith was probably having the same dream I'd had. I hid my head under my pillow. I really hated to see my brother looking so happy.

To punish Keith for stealing my goal, I didn't wake him up like I usually did. Keith always sleeps through the alarm. My dad says that Keith could sleep through a rock concert, even if the group was a heavy metal band and it was playing at the foot of his bed. I left my brother snoring away and took Elvis for his morning walk.

Elvis and I have two routes for his morning walk. If it's nice and we have time, we take the long one. The long one goes up to the end of our street, over the foot-bridge, and down the other side of the railway tracks and back again. If it's raining or I'm in a hurry, we just go once round the block.

It was a nice day, and I was still upset about my dream, so Elvis and I took the long route. He stopped every three centimetres to sniff something, so I had plenty of time to think about Keith stealing my goal like that.

The weird thing about my dream was that I don't even play football. I mean, I play football, but not for real. I just fool around on the heath

after school with Midge. Midge is my best mate. I'm not very good at football, but Midge is worse. I'm always picked second or next to last for teams, but Midge is always picked last. Most of the time when we do play a game, nobody will pass Midge the ball unless they have absolutely no choice, because he always fumbles or falls over or something. Even though the one time I ever scored was an accident, at least I managed to get the ball in the right goal. The only time Midge ever scored, he won the game for the other team.

Keith is brilliant at football. He's on a team with real uniforms and real games and real trophies. He was even trying for a place on a junior British team that was going to Europe. He had his photo in the local paper when his team won the area league championship. The caption underneath said: *A Future Pro?* Keith's grinning like he just won the Cup Final. He's got the picture on the pin-board over his desk. It made me want to puke. The only picture on my pin-board was of Elvis the time he got stuck up a tree. I taped a piece of paper to it that said: Bird Dog.

The worst thing is, Keith isn't just good at football, he's good at all sports. He swims, he plays rugby, he skates, he runs, he even does gymnastics. You'd think he was in training to be a superhero. You know, in case Batman came down with the flu. My mum says Keith's just very physical. As if I hadn't noticed. I'm the one he was always beating up.

My mum said that wasn't what she meant. She meant that Keith is a natural athlete. Some people are. And some people aren't.

'You mean like me,' I said.

My mum patted me on the head the same way she pats Elvis. 'You're good at other things,' she assured me. 'You have your own special talents.' She didn't say what.

So that morning Elvis and I were walking along, him sniffing and me trying to think of all the things I was good at, when I realized we were right outside Mrs Lim's house. I'd been so busy brooding about Keith that I'd forgotten about Mrs Lim. And about Honey, her big ginger cat. Elvis hates Honey. Honey doesn't like him much either. That's why I usually make sure we walk on the opposite pavement. But this morning I forgot.

'Uh oh,' I said to Elvis. 'We better get out of here before Mrs Lim sees us.'

But it was already too late. Honey was on the window-sill. Her fur was standing up so much she looked like she'd been pumped full of air, and she was making this sound between a growl and lift-off. Elvis started barking and trying to walk on his back legs.

'Come on, Elvis,' I grunted. I dug in my heels and pulled on his lead with all my strength. 'Come on, boy. Let's go home. Don't you want breakfast?'

But the only thing Elvis wanted to eat right then was Honey. He was trying to drag me to the window.

'Please, Elvis,' I begged. 'You can have toast and marmalade if you'll come home now.' Elvis loves toast and marmalade. He was still pulling forward, but his ears went up at the mention of marmalade. 'Extra marmalade,' I promised. 'Extra marmalade and lots of butter.'

I really think he would have let me take him home then if Honey hadn't begun to yowl. It was the creepiest thing I'd ever heard. Like something out of *Poltergeist*. You know, like some deranged demon had taken over Honey's body. Elvis thought it was creepy too, because that was when he lost it completely.

It's lucky Mrs Lim has a hedge in front of her house. It slowed Elvis down enough so Mrs Lim had time to get to the door before he actually jumped on her cat. Mrs Lim opened the door just as Elvis yanked the lead out of my hand and hurled himself at the window-sill. Sounding like she was being sucked into a sea of ectoplasm, Honey shot past Mrs Lim. Elvis ran after her.

Mrs Lim was already screaming at me. 'Do

something, Adam Wiggins!' she was screaming. 'Stop that dog!'

I did something. I went after Elvis. Only I didn't go along the pavement to the front door like I should have. I panicked. Mrs Lim was carrying on like the Hound from Hell was after her, and Elvis and Honey were going ballistic. The three of them were making such a racket that I decided to take the short cut – through the hedge.

Mrs Lim's hedge came up to my chest. I reckoned I could jump over it, the way Elvis had. I jumped. It's a good thing I'm thin, or it might have been worse. I might have been the first boy in Britain to drown in shrubbery. Because I didn't clear the hedge like Elvis, I landed in the middle of it.

Mrs Lim was still screaming. 'Do you hear me, Adam Wiggins? Get that monster out of my house!'

I tried to pull myself out, but my foot was jammed in these branches and there were all these other branches poking into me, making it hard to move. 'I can't,' I yelled back. 'I'm stuck!'

Mrs Lim was waving her hands in the air. 'What's wrong with your parents, putting a little boy like you in charge of a creature like that?' Mrs Lim screeched. 'Don't they have any sense?

Your brother's the one who should be walking that dog. Your brother could control him.'

And then she ran back into the house to rescue Honey, and I had to get out of the hedge by myself.

Chapter Two

I was afraid I was going to miss Midge. We always meet on his corner and go to school together, but this morning I was late because of what Elvis and Honey did to Mrs Lim's kitchen. Mrs Lim said it reminded her of war-torn Saigon. She wouldn't let me go home till I helped her clean up. She said it was the least I could do. And then, when I did go home, my mum made me wash off Elvis and put antiseptic on my scratches from the hedge before she'd let me leave the house again. Midge was there waiting for me, though. He was looking at his watch, but he was there.

'What happened to you?' he wanted to know. 'I was just about to go on my own.'

I ran up to him. 'You won't believe it. I've only been awake about an hour and I've already had one of the worst days of my life.'

I told Midge what had happened while we

walked to school. First I told him about my dream. 'Nightmare, more like,' I told him.

Midge sympathized. 'I pity you,' said Midge. 'It's bad enough having Keith around when you're awake. I'd hate to have him around in my sleep too.'

Then I told him about Mrs Lim.

'You should've heard her, Midge.' My voice squeaked, I was that upset. Usually I'll shut up if my voice is squeaking because Keith says I sound like a girl. But today I didn't care. 'It isn't fair,' I squeaked some more. 'I get the blame and it's all Keith's fault.'

It really was all Keith's fault. He thinks it's funny to get me in trouble so he's always playing these dumb jokes. That's why Elvis hates Honey so much. Keith used to sneak Honey down to our house and hold her up outside the front window. 'Elvis!' he'd call, all nice and sweet. 'Elvis, there's somebody here to see you.' Elvis would go berserk, and Keith would just about wet himself laughing. Keith only stopped doing that because once Elvis went through the window. The vet said Elvis would have been hurt if he hadn't been going so fast. I got the blame that time, too.

'Mrs Lim wouldn't stop raving about what a credit to my parents Keith is and how I should try to be more like him,' I went on.

Midge understood. He knows my brother almost as well as I do. 'It's like telling somebody to be more like Frankenstein's monster,' he said.

'Even after I helped her straighten up the kitchen, she was still screaming at me. She wouldn't shut up about how I'm so little and weak, and how it's too bad I don't take after Keith.' I kicked a stone across the street. It stopped in the middle of the road. 'Sometimes I really wish Keith had never been born. Then nobody could compare me to him all the time.'

Midge stopped sympathizing. 'It's only Mrs Lim,' said Midge. 'Who cares what she thinks? Her cat smells like rotten cheese.'

'It's not just Mrs Lim,' I argued. 'It's everyone.'

'No it isn't,' said Midge. 'It's only Mrs Lim and you. You're the one who's always comparing you to Keith. I think you're getting a complex about him.'

I gave Midge a look. Midge has been my best friend for ever, but he can be really annoying when he wants to be. And sometimes he doesn't even have to want to – he just is.

'You mean like you've got a complex about being short?' I snapped back.

Midge pushed his glasses up his nose. 'That's different, Adam. I *am* short. But just because you're not like Keith doesn't mean there's anything wrong with you.' He shook his head. 'Be logical, will you?' Midge is into logic. He's very brainy. 'It'd be pretty weird if Keith wasn't bigger and stronger and could play football better. He's thirteen and you're only eight.'

I could be logical too. 'But that's not the point, is it?' I asked. I got another stone into position. This time I was aiming at this one leaf a few metres ahead of us.

Midge's eyebrows rose over the rims of his glasses. 'What is the point then?'

I made my kick. I hit a tree. 'The point is that for my whole life I'm always going to be Keith Wiggins' brother. No matter what I do, or where I go, I'll always have to live with that.'

'So?' Midge demanded. 'That's not so bad. My whole life I'm never going to be anybody's brother.'

Boo hoo. Midge isn't just an only child, he's also adopted. I couldn't see that he had anything to complain about. Knowing you were never going to have a brother like Keith was even better than not having one.

'I'll tell you what's so bad,' I said. I jammed my hands into my pockets. 'It's like always being Robin, that's what's so bad. No matter how hard I try, I'll never be Batman. I'll never get to drive the Batmobile. I'll never outsmart the

Penguin. I'll always be the little bloke in the green tights who says dumb things and never knows what's going on.'

Midge groaned. 'You're going over the top as usual, Adam,' said Midge. 'I'll admit Keith's better at some things than you are, but that's no big deal. There are tons of things you're good at that Keith is lousy at.'

He sounded like my mother.

'Yeah?'

Midge nodded. 'Yeah.'

I waited to hear all the things I was good at that Keith was lousy at. Midge didn't say anything. 'Like what?' I finally asked.

'Like what?' Midge pretended he was thinking really hard. He scratched his hair and puckered his forehead. 'Well . . .' he said. He sighed. 'There must be something . . .'

I gave him a shove. 'Get off,' I said.

'No, really, Adam.' He shoved me back. 'I'm sure there must be something.'

We were still laughing and shoving each other when we saw these three boys cycling towards us. They were about Keith's age. We'd seen them around before. They were the sort of boys who pick on kids who are smaller and stuff like that. You could tell just by the way they walked down the street that they were trouble. They were laughing, too, but it wasn't a very happy sound. I knew right away that they were laughing at us. So did Midge.

'I suppose it's too late to cross over now?' he whispered.

'I think so,' I whispered back. We didn't want them to think we were afraid of them. They were also the sort of boys who would love the idea that you were afraid of them.

'Well, look who's here,' said the biggest of the three. 'If it isn't Dopey and Sleepy.'

They came to a stop about a metre in front of us, blocking our way. The one facing me was tall and thin and his hair was cut so short it was hard to tell what colour it was. The one facing Midge was tall and chubby and had almost black hair and really light-blue eyes. The one in the middle was the biggest. He wasn't just tall, he was broad and solid and had a scar over his right eye. He looked like he was going to be Arnold Schwarzenegger when he grew up. Only meaner.

Midge moved to the right and I moved to the left, but the boys on the outside moved with us. The one in the middle just smiled.

'Not so fast,' said the boy in the middle. He had a lot of thick blond hair and small, cold eyes. I didn't think much of his smile.

I glanced at Midge. 'We're in a hurry,' I said, praying I wouldn't squeak. 'We have to get to school.'

That made all three of them smirk.

'We have to get to school, too,' said the boy in the middle. 'Only we have a problem, don't we?' He shook his head sadly. 'My mates and me, we lost our dinner money.' He made a big thing of looking us up and down. 'Unlike you two, we're growing boys. We need to eat regular. We can't go to school without any dinner money, can we?'

Midge glanced at me. 'I'm sorry we can't help you,' he said. He touched my arm really lightly. 'But we have to get going or we'll be late.'

We took another step forward.

The boy in front of Midge put his hand on Midge's shoulder. 'Why don't you give us *your* dinner money?' he asked in this quiet voice. Psycho-killers in films always talk like that. He brushed something off Midge's collar. 'Then I won't have to mess up your nice school uniform by taking it from you.'

Midge isn't the smartest kid in our class for nothing. 'I don't have any dinner money,' he answered quickly. He held up his satchel. 'I bring a packed lunch.'

The tall, thin boy put his hand out to me. 'What about you?' he asked, grabbing hold of my jacket. 'You look like the sort of mummy's boy who always has money.' He twisted my jacket so hard I thought I was going to choke.

I had almost a whole week's pocket money with me because I didn't like to leave it at home in case my brother decided to 'borrow' some. He was always doing stuff like that.

'No,' I said. I was squeaking. Even I could hear that I sounded just like a girl. 'No, I don't have any money. I bring a packed lunch, too.'

'Really?' With the hand that wasn't trying to strangle me, he shook my jacket. It jingled. 'What's that then? You carry bits of metal around with you?' He smiled some more. He had an awful lot of teeth. He reached in my pocket and came out with a handful of coins. 'I hate little nerds who lie to me,' he said.

My brother wouldn't have been scared by these yobs. My brother wouldn't have wanted to cry. My brother would have slapped that creep's hand from his jacket. He would have grabbed back his pocket money and then he would have shoved him out of his way. Boy, did I wish I was my brother.

I don't know if I really would have cried right then or if I would have waited till after they'd gone, but right at that second two women came out of the house beside us. The thin creep let go of me. All five of us watched the women come down the path. One of them had a baby in a buggy. The baby was stuffing something into its face, and the women were chatting away. The one who wasn't pushing the buggy opened the front gate. Midge and I looked at each other.

'Wow,' I said, practically shouting, 'what a nice baby.'

Midge waggled his fingers at the baby. 'Hi,' he said. 'What's your name?'

Chewed-up biscuit dribbled down the baby's chin. The women sort of smiled at us vaguely and turned to walk past. Not looking at the other boys, Midge and I went with them.

As soon as we got to the corner, we started to run.

'I'm really glad I waited for you,' Midge said as we turned into the road our school is on.

'I'm glad you waited, too,' I said. The bell went. We sped up.

'What would I have done if I'd been on my own?' asked Midge.

And what would I have done if I'd been on my own?

It was a good question.

Chapter Three

You'd think a day that started with your dog landing in Mrs Lim's breakfast and someone threatening your life couldn't get any worse, wouldn't you? I mean, if you'd had to scrape the strawberry jam off Elvis's ears or if you'd seen the look in those creeps' eyes, you'd have reckoned you'd hit the bottom. *This is it*, you'd have said to yourself. *Things can only get better from now on.*

But you'd have been wrong.

The only people still in the playground when we finally got to school were pigeons.

'I don't believe this,' I said to Midge. 'Why is this happening to me? Now we're going to get into trouble for being late.' We raced through the gates.

'There you go again, right over the top,' panted Midge. He's short, so he has to run twice as fast. 'You know Mrs Vorha. If we act like we've been there all the time, she won't even notice.'

I know I get carried away with myself now and then. My mum says it's because I have a very active imagination. My brother says it's because I'm crazy. 'If Adam was a bike he'd only have one wheel,' Keith always says. He thinks he's a riot.

I took the steps two at a time. 'Maybe you're right,' I said. After all, it always took a few minutes for the class to settle down and Mrs Vorha usually spent those few minutes writing stuff on the board or pulling dead leaves off the plants on the window-sill. If we slipped in quietly and went straight to our seats, she probably wouldn't say anything even if she did notice. I opened the door.

There was usually a lot of noise while everyone was settling down, but today the room was silent. Or almost silent. One voice was speaking. One deep, male voice.

'I'd like to thank you two gentlemen for deciding to join us,' said the voice.

I was so surprised, I stopped dead. I'd forgotten we were having a substitute for a few days because Mrs Vorha had some special conference on education to go to.

Midge had forgotten, too. He ploughed right into me. I sort of tripped into the room and landed on Jasmine Nejari's desk. Jasmine's one of these girls who always has a lot of things on her desk. Not just things you're supposed to have on your desk, like pens and paper and books, but all sorts of little pretty things in pastel colours. It all went flying. Jasmine hit me over the head with this pink ruler with kittens on it. 'You idiot!' she shrieked. 'Now look what you've done. You're going to pick it all up.'

Everyone who wasn't laughing already started laughing then. I could even hear Midge's giggle. Midge's giggle sounds like someone spitting out a mouthful of water. The only person who didn't think it was totally hilarious was the teacher who wasn't Mrs Vorha. I could feel him glaring at me while I crawled around on the floor.

Finally, I found the last two things – a rubber that looked like a rabbit and a star-shaped sharpener – and got to my feet.

'If you think you've disrupted this class enough for one morning, perhaps you'd sit down now,' said the substitute.

'Yes, Sir.' I dumped the rabbit and the star on Jasmine's desk and collapsed in my chair.

The substitute picked up the register, his beady eyes going down the page. 'And you are . . .?' he asked.

'Adam,' I mumbled. 'Adam Wiggins.'

'Wiggins?' He raised his head. 'Adam *Wiggins*?' You'd think he'd never seen an eight-year-old boy before, the way he was looking at me.

'*You're* not Keith Wiggins' *brother*, are you?'

I could tell it wasn't really a question.

No, I felt like saying. *I'm his sister.*

I don't remember much of what we did in school that day, because I was too busy brooding about Keith. When I thought it over, it seemed to me that people were always saying, '*You're* Keith Wiggins' brother?' Like they couldn't believe we came from the same planet, never mind the same parents. Every time I got a new teacher, or tried for a team, or joined a club, or went some place where Keith was known, I always got the same reaction. Whoever it was would look at me for a few seconds and then he'd shake his head like he must have misheard me, and then he say, 'Wiggins? You mean *you're* related to *Keith Wiggins?*'

I was still brooding when we got out of school. On Wednesdays me and Midge usually go up to the heath to play football or just muck about. This was a Wednesday so we headed to my house to collect Elvis and the ball.

'It's just that I'm really tired of everybody acting so surprised when they find out I'm Keith's brother,' I complained as we walked along. We were taking the long way back to Chester Crescent just in case those boys were waiting for us. Midge and I hadn't said anything about it, but we'd both automatically gone straight out of the gates instead of turning right the way we usually did.

'You mean like the substitute?' asked Midge.

'No,' I said. 'Like everyone.'

'I wouldn't let Mr Altman get to you.' Midge offered me the packet of crisps he'd saved from lunch. 'He only acted like that because we were late.' He bit into a crisp, chewing slowly. 'And because you made such a spectacle of yourself.' He glanced over. 'Didn't I tell you to sit down quietly? You know what substitutes are like. They have to prove they're in control right away or they might as well go home.'

Personally, I wished Mr Altman had gone home. 'He didn't act like that because we were late,' I said. 'He acted like that because he thinks Keith's Superman and I'm Daffy Duck.'

It turned out that Mr Altman knew my brother really well. Mr Altman taught Keith's class for a couple of months when the real teacher was having a baby. All day, Mr Altman had called on me every chance he got, and every time he did he found some reason for mentioning my brother and how I was nothing like him. Keith never disrupted the class. Keith always paid attention. Keith would have known what the capital of Canada was. Mr Altman liked Keith almost as much as Keith liked Keith.

'You're exaggerating again,' said Midge. 'Mr Altman doesn't think you're Daffy Duck. Donald, maybe, but not Daffy.'

'Oh ha ha ha,' I said. 'Maybe you should become a comedian if you ever grow up.'

It was a warm, sunny day, so the heath was really crowded. There must've been about a million people playing ball and flying kites and throwing frisbees at each other. Elvis is all right with footballs because they're too big for him to fit in his mouth, but you have to watch him with frisbees. One time Midge and I spent an hour running round a pond, trying to get this little kid's frisbee back, and when we finally did, it had all these teeth marks on it. So instead of playing ball, we decided to walk where there weren't so many people.

There are a lot of fun things in the woods on the heath. Elvis likes to sniff around for rabbits and birds, and Midge and I like to explore. There's a stream and a couple of ponds and a lot of fallen trees you can climb over. There's even this old hollow tree that's so big you can get inside it. That afternoon we pretended the hollow tree was a starship and that we were intergalactic policemen hurtling through space on a secret mission. By the time we were ready to head for home, I was in a pretty good mood.

'Let's go out by the café and get an ice-cream,' I suggested. I was off the path, hunting for another stick to throw for Elvis. Elvis loves chasing sticks but he doesn't understand that he's supposed to bring them back.

'Adam,' said Midge.

'My treat.'

I could feel Midge come closer to me. 'Adam, look over there.'

I didn't turn around. 'Just a second,' I said. 'If I can get a couple of sticks I won't have to stop again.'

'*Now*, Adam.' Midge kicked me.

I turned round. I looked. Three boys on mountain bikes were coming down the hill.

'So?' I said. Lots of people cycle on the heath even though you're not supposed to.

'Don't you recognize them?' asked Midge.

I looked again. The boy on the green bike was thin. The boy on the pink-and-yellow bike was chubby. The boy on the black bike looked like he might be the Terminator when he was a kid, or maybe just the son of the Terminator. They were pedalling even though they could have free-wheeled.

'It's *them*!' hissed Midge, just in case I hadn't caught on yet. 'The teenagers from hell.'

I don't suppose it really mattered whether I recognized them or not, because it was obvious the way they were grinning and pedalling like mad that they recognized us.

'Well, look who's here!' shouted the one on the black bike. 'If it isn't our little friends from this morning, Dopey and Sleepy.'

'You owe us some money,' the one on the green bike was screaming.

'With interest!' the chubby one chimed in.

Midge was so close to me by now, if I'd moved he would have fallen over. 'What are we going to do?' he whispered. I was glad he sounded as scared as I felt.

I glanced round. Except for Elvis, who was sitting in front of me, wagging his tail while he waited for me to throw him a stick, we were surrounded by trees. There wasn't a woman with a buggy in sight. No one was going to rescue us this time.

'There's only one thing we can do,' I whispered back. I reckoned even twenty-one-gear mountain bikes would have trouble cutting through the woods. 'Run.'

Being faster than Midge, I took the lead. I could hear Midge panting and wheezing behind me, but I didn't look back. I just kept going. Elvis passed me, barking and bouncing. He thought it was a game. Suddenly I didn't hear Midge any more. Instead, all I could hear were thick rubber tyres crunching over twigs and leaves and voices screaming, 'Get him! Get him! Get him!' I still didn't look round. I didn't want to know how close they were. I was so scared even my feet were sweating.

Head for the trees! I told myself. *Head for the trees!*

I headed for the trees.

The teenagers from hell headed for the trees, too. I was wrong about how much trouble mountain bikes would have getting through the woods. They didn't have that much trouble at all.

I'd never run so fast or so hard in my life. It felt like my heart was going to punch its way out of my chest. I wished Keith could see me. He wouldn't believe it. And I would have made it, too, if it weren't for Elvis. He was so excited that he started running round me in circles.

'Get out of the way!' I gasped. 'Elvis, get out of the way!'

He must have thought I was calling him or something, because instead of getting out of the way he stopped dead. But I didn't. It was like hitting a log. I flew over Elvis and landed head-first in a bush for the second time that day. I was already tired of it.

That cracked them up.

'Enjoy your trip, Dopey?' one of them gasped.

Then this hand grabbed hold of me and hauled me to my feet. It was the big one with

31

the lousy personality. 'You shouldn't have run like that, you little nerd,' he said in this soft, threatening voice. 'Now I'm going to have to teach you a lesson.'

He's going to hit me, I thought. *He's going to hit me and I'm going to cry.*

I watched his arm pull back. I watched his fist come forward. For the rest of my life, every time I saw this creep he'd call me cry-baby and hit me.

And then Elvis went mad.

'What happened to you two?' asked my mother.

Midge and I stopped so fast we bumped into each other. I hadn't seen my mother lurking on the stairs. I thought she was in another part of the house and we'd be able to sneak up to the bathroom and clean up before she saw us. I should be so lucky. Sometimes I think my mum has radar.

'Us?' I asked.

'Hi, Mrs Wiggins,' said Midge.

My mum smiled at Midge. 'Hello, Jerome.' But she didn't smile at me. 'Yes, you,' said my mum. 'You're filthy.'

'We were fooling around on the heath,' I said. I prayed she hadn't noticed that I was limping a little. I must have twisted my ankle when I fell over Elvis.

She came down the last few steps. She made the same sound she made the time she found the slug in her salad. 'Look at you!' She was practically shouting. 'Both of you are covered in scratches.'

This was an exaggeration. Maybe I was sort of covered in scratches because first I'd landed in Mrs Lim's hedge and then I'd landed in that dumb bush, but Midge wasn't. All Midge had was a couple of tiny cuts from climbing up a tree to get away from the bikers.

'It's from this morning,' I said. 'Remember?'

'You didn't have that many scratches this morning.' My mum was staring at me so hard I almost thought she was counting them. She brought her face right up to mine. 'Some of those scratches are fresh,' she said. She turned to Midge. 'And so are the ones on Jerome.'

I grabbed Midge's sleeve and started edging past her. 'I told you,' I said. 'We were fooling around on the heath.'

My mother shifted to the left. 'Fooling around doing what?'

I shrugged. Midge shrugged. We'd agreed that we wouldn't tell my mother what had happened because she'd only get all worried and upset, but we hadn't actually agreed on what we would tell her.

'Well?' said my mother. 'Fooling around doing what?'

Midge smiled. I smiled. 'Just fooling around.'

Elvis and I stopped in the doorway to the living-room. My parents were sitting on the couch, watching television, and Keith was on the floor doing push-ups. 'Good-night,' I said.

My mum and dad looked up, but Keith just kept counting under his breath.

'Don't tell me you're going to bed already,' said my mother. 'It's not even nine yet.'

I yawned. 'I'm really knackered,' I said. Which was true. Running for your life can really whack you out.

My mother looked like she was thinking of taking my temperature. 'I hope you're not coming down with something,' she said. 'You don't think any of those scratches are infected, do you?'

'I'm fine, Mum.' She'd put enough antiseptic on me to disinfect a hospital. I yawned again. 'I've had a very exhausting day.'

'I know,' said my mother. 'Fooling around.'

'Weakling,' muttered my brother. He was in the eighties but he wasn't even out of breath.

'I am not a weakling,' I protested. 'I'm tired, that's all.'

'And so you should be,' said my brother, still counting. 'Destroying Mrs Lim's kitchen must've taken every ounce of strength you've got.'

If I hadn't been so tired I would have thrown something at him.

'Stop it, Keith,' said my father. 'Good-night, Adam.'

I shut the door.

Besides being tired and hurting in about sixty different places, I wanted to go to bed early so I could be alone to think. The only time you get any privacy in my house is when you're in the loo or everybody believes you're asleep.

I was already thinking as I got into my pyjamas. When Keith was my age, he was always getting into fights. Now he never got into fights because he was so strong nobody wanted to fight him. I turned out the light. And he was a football star. Nobody bullies a football star. I pulled down the blankets. My parents only had two children. That meant I'd had a fifty-fifty chance of being the natural athlete, the one who was very physical. But I wasn't. I was the unnatural athlete, the one who wasn't good at physical things. I was the wimp. I got into bed. It should have been the other way round. Keith should have been the one who got stuck in Mrs Lim's hedge. I screamed.

I didn't mean to scream, but I couldn't help it. My feet had touched something warm and mushy. Something disgusting. I could smell it. This was just what I needed. First the dream.

Then Mrs Lim and Honey. Then the teenagers from hell. Then Mr Altman. And now this. Vomit. The perfect end to a horrible day. My brother had thrown up in my bed. I was still screaming as I threw off the blankets and landed on the floor.

And then I heard it. The unmistakable sound of Keith William Wiggins wetting himself laughing.

'I'll get you for this!' I screamed. 'I mean it, you android. I'll get you for this.'

'You and whose army?' The light went on. Keith was leaning against the door, doubled up. Tears were running down his cheeks.

I looked at my feet. There was dog food all over my toes.

'Serves you right for not waking me up this morning,' said my brother. 'I was nearly late for school.'

I should have known he'd get even with me for that. My brother never lets me get away with anything.

Chapter Four

My dad had left for work and Keith and his best friend, Charlie Donaldson, were doing a few hundred laps in the pool before school, so my mum and I were having breakfast by ourselves.

'Mum,' I said. 'Mum, if you could only have had one child, which one of us would you have picked?'

She looked at me. I almost thought she was going to laugh. 'What's brought this on?' she asked.

I carefully buttered my toast. 'Nothing,' I said. 'I was just wondering, that's all.'

She put down the teapot. 'You were just wondering.'

'Uh huh.' I nodded. Our eyes met. My mum has this way of looking at you as if she can read your mind. It makes it hard to keep secrets from her. I smiled in what I hoped was an encouraging way. 'You know,' I said.

My mother didn't know.

'Why would you wonder about a thing like

that?' Her eyes narrowed and she squeezed her lips together, which isn't a good sign. It means she's thinking. 'What's Keith been telling you this time?'

'Nothing, Mum.' I reckoned she must be thinking of the time Keith told me I was adopted and that if I didn't shape up my foster-parents were going to give me back. 'I was just wondering, that's all. I mean, what if God told you you could only have one son, which of us would you have wanted it to be?'

She wasn't thinking of the time Keith convinced me I was adopted.

Her eyes narrowed even more. 'He didn't tell you your father lost his job and we have to put one of you in a home again, did he?'

'No, Mum, it's nothing like that.' I was really sorry I'd opened my mouth. I should have known she wouldn't tell me the truth.

'Because it's a ridiculous question,' my mother was saying. 'You know your father and I love both of you the same.'

'But you can't,' I said. This was the last thought I had just before I finally fell asleep the night before – that not only did Keith do everything better than I did, and not only did teachers and other grown-ups like Keith better than they liked me, but that my parents couldn't love us equally the way they were always saying they

did. 'We're completely different. You have to like one of us more than the other.'

'Of course you're completely different.' My mother leaned towards me. She was looking very sincere. She always looks sincere when she doesn't want to hurt my feelings. 'That's why we don't have a favourite.'

I wasn't sure I followed that. It seemed to me that if two things were so different, you were bound to like one more than the other. You know, I like peanut butter and I like chocolate, but I like chocolate more than I like peanut butter. 'But Keith's stronger than I am, and smarter than I am, and better at sports –'

My mother interrupted me. 'And you have a lot of terrific qualities and abilities that Keith doesn't have.'

'Like what?' I suppose I was hoping she'd say, *like a great personality* or even, *you're a lot nicer.*

She picked up her mug. 'Like an overactive imagination,' said my mother.

'What are you doing?' asked Midge.

I looked up. He was lifting the top of his sandwich to check that his mother hadn't stuck something into it that he didn't like. 'I'm making a list.'

Satisfied that there was nothing in there but tuna salad and some dead lettuce, Midge took a bite. 'What kind of list?'

I put down my pencil. 'It's a list of all the things Keith can do that I can't do, and all the things I can do that Keith can't do.'

Midge chewed slowly. 'I was right,' he said. 'You are getting a complex. Maybe you should talk to my mum.' Midge's mother is a psychotherapist.

'I don't need to talk to your mother.' Talking to my mother was bad enough. Midge couldn't forget to empty the rubbish without Mrs Greaves coming up with at least six different reasons why he hadn't remembered.

Midge pulled his chair around the table so he was sitting beside me. 'What have you got so far?'

I showed him what I had so far.

Things Keith Does Better:
Football
Swimming
Rugby
Running
Gymnastics
Fighting
Wrestling
Science
Maths
Making stuff
Fixing things
Ruining my life

Things I Do Better:
Being tidy
Making my bed
Helping around the house

Midge sipped his juice. 'There isn't much in your column,' he pointed out.

Like he needed to. Like I didn't know there wasn't much in my column.

'Oh, really,' I said. 'How come I didn't notice that?'

The trouble was that the more I'd thought about it, the more I'd realized that it wasn't just that Keith could do things that I couldn't do. It was that anything I *could* do, he did better. I reckoned that even if me and Keith were the same age, I'd still be smaller and weaker. Even if I was older than Keith, he'd still be good at football and stuff like that and I wouldn't. Even if Keith was five, he wouldn't have let Elvis pull the lead out of his hand. I was lucky I'd come up with as much as I had. At first the only thing I could think of was that I don't have any fillings in my teeth and my brother does.

'You don't have to get an attitude,' said Midge. He put down the sandwich. 'What about writing?' he suggested. 'Mrs Vorha really liked that essay you did on being someone else.'

It was true, Mrs Vorha had liked my essay. She'd liked it so much she even entered it in this competition one of the big biscuit companies was running to encourage children to write creatively. We had to put ourselves in someone else's shoes. A lot of the girls pretended they were

models or actresses, and most of the boys pretended they were pop stars or football players.
My essay was about what it would be like if I
couldn't walk and had to go around in a wheel-
chair. I got the idea from a documentary on the
telly that I watched with my dad. I made Midge
pull me around in my old go-kart after school
every day for a week, so I could really see what
it was like. It was horrible. I couldn't go into
shops, or go up steps, or anything. I stopped
counting how many times I fell out going over
a kerb. Mrs Vorha said my essay was the best
in the class. She said it wasn't only very well
written but that it showed a lot of sensitivity
too.

'I don't know,' I said. 'I don't think Keith
cares if he can write or not.' Not the way I
wished I could play football. 'Do you reckon it
still counts?'

Midge nodded. 'Sure,' he said. He bit into his
sandwich again. 'And anyway, Adam, you have
to put down something.'

Midge and I had ridden our bikes to school that
morning even though it was raining. We thought
we were pretty clever. That way, even if we did
run into those bullies, we'd be able to get away
from them. We might get soaked, but we were
guaranteed to be in one piece.

It was still raining hard when we came out of school that afternoon, which meant that pavement was slick and slippery, so we decided to walk. Since it was a Thursday we were going to my house. We automatically took the long route, even though it was unlikely that they'd be standing in a downpour, waiting for us. Nobody was that crazy, not even this lot.

'Maybe we shouldn't have run like that, yesterday,' Midge said as we pushed our bikes through the gates of the school. I knew what he was thinking. He was thinking: *Keith wouldn't have run . . .*

'Oh, right.' I made a face. 'Maybe we should've stayed there and let them mug us. Then they could've taken your money, too.'

Midge gave me a look back. 'We could've stood up to them,' he suggested. *Keith would have stood up to them.*

I could hardly believe my ears. Midge is Midge's nickname. There's a very good reason why his nickname isn't the Incredible Hulk.

'And we could have been pulverized,' I pointed out. I didn't bother mentioning that he was the one who climbed the tree.

Midge shrugged. 'Maybe.' *Keith wouldn't have been pulverized.*

'*Maybe?* You mean like *maybe* the sky isn't blue?'

Midge was watching the pavement. 'It's just that they won't leave us alone now that they know we're afraid of them.' *Keith wouldn't be afraid.*

I wished Midge would stop thinking about Keith. I wished I would, too.

'They already knew we were afraid of them,' I reminded him. 'And anyway, they came after us, Midge. And that big one was going to hit me. Hard. That isn't what I call leaving someone alone.'

We turned the corner.

'Yeah,' Midge mumbled, 'but my mum says you don't solve problems by running away from them. My mum says that only way to solve a problem is to stand up to it.'

All of a sudden, I stopped thinking about my brother. I grabbed hold of Midge's arm. 'It's too bad your mother isn't here right now, then,' I said.

'Ow,' said Midge. 'You're hurt—'

And then he saw what I saw. Down the street, facing in the direction we should have been coming from, were the teenagers from hell. Even though it was pouring down, they looked really happy. You know, the way sharks look happy when they smell blood.

'They've got their bikes!' As if I hadn't noticed. Midge turned to me. 'Now what are we going to do?' There was nobody else around, but he was whispering.

'I thought we were going to stand up to them,' I answered. 'Isn't that what you wanted to do? Isn't that the only way to solve our problem?'

'It's too late for that,' said Midge. 'Now that we've already run away from them they have a psychological advantage.'

I stared at the three boys. They were goofing around, laughing and hitting each other while they waited for me and Midge. The smallest one was twice the size of Midge. All the chubby one would have to do was sit on us. I didn't even like to think about the one who looked like Arnold Schwarzenegger.

'They have more than a psychological advantage,' I said. 'They're well bigger than we are, too.'

Midge sighed. 'You know what I wish?' he asked.

I looked around, trying to decide which direction we should take. If we went back to the school, we could loop around and come out a few streets from where the teenage mutant thugs were waiting for us. If we went left, we could take the underpass and come out on the other side of the motorway.

'That we came from Krypton?' I answered. It was what I was wishing.

'No,' said Midge. 'I wish your brother was here.'

'Thanks a lot.' If he wasn't my best friend, I would have hit him. 'I thought you were supposed to be on my side. I thought you were supposed to be boosting my ego, making me feel better . . .'

Midge made a gargling sound. I took this to mean that he thought he was on my side.

'No you're not,' I went on. 'If you really were on my side you wouldn't wish that Keith was here. You'd be happy he isn't. You —'

Midge got his voice back. 'Get on your bike, Adam!' he screamed. 'They've seen us! They're coming! Get on your bike!'

I looked round. They had seen us and they were coming. A little thing like a slippery pavement wasn't going to stop these kids. A blizzard wouldn't have stopped them.

Midge was already on his bike. 'Adam!' he was shouting. 'Adam, come on!'

At least it solved the problem of which way we were going. There wasn't any time to turn back towards the school. We were going straight ahead, down the underpass.

The rain was in our favour. It might not have stopped them, but it slowed them down a lot. They were having trouble trying to catch up.

Midge disappeared down the underpass. I followed.

We both screamed 'Look out!' at the same time. Right ahead with their backs to us, was a woman with two little kids walking beside her.

At the sound of our voices they all stopped dead. Midge hit his brakes and I ran into the back of him.

The little kids started crying and the woman started screaming, but up at the top of the ramp I could hear three teenage terrorists laughing hysterically.

'Hey, Dopey!' one of them was shouting. 'Don't you ever get tired of falling down?'

Chapter Five

I leaned over the banister and looked into the kitchen. My brother was sitting at the table, reading a comic while he shovelled cereal into his gob. My mother was standing with her back to me, putting bread in the toaster. With a little luck, I could get to the front door without them seeing me.

My brother heard me the second my feet touched the hall. 'Where are you going?' he asked in this loud voice. He didn't even glance up from his comic.

When she heard Keith, my mother turned from the toaster with a slice of bread in her hand. She wasn't too pleased with me at the moment because I came home with my trousers ripped and my bike broken. The frame got sort of bent when I hit Midge. My mum said I had to pay for the repairs myself. Which meant my bike would never get fixed, because every time I had some money those boys were going to take it from me. Keith said it was too bad I was useless or I could fix the bike myself.

'It's Friday morning, isn't it?' I made a face that said I thought it was pretty weird that anyone should wonder what I was doing. 'I'm going to school.'

'Hey, you're improving, Adam,' said my brother through another mouthful of cornflakes. 'You actually know what day it is. We'll teach you to tell the time next.'

'Shhh, Keith,' said my mum. She was staring hard at me, trying to read my mind again. '*Now?*' She waved the bread at me. 'Isn't it a little early for you to be going to school?'

It was a little early. It was forty-three minutes early, to be exact. But Midge and I had come up with a plan for living until Saturday. The first part of the plan was avoidance. If we didn't run into those boys, they couldn't hurt us. That's why we'd decided to leave for school earlier than we usually did. If we'd had to leave for school at dawn, we would have.

I concentrated on not looking guilty and on not looking into the eyes of Caroline Wiggins, Detective Inspector. 'We've got some stuff to do before school starts,' I said. Which was true. We had to survive.

D. I. Wiggins drew her eyebrows together. 'I thought you said you were late getting home last night because you had stuff to do after school.' Didn't she ever forget anything?

'I did,' I said. In the end, we'd walked along with the woman and her kids till we were sure the teenage terrorists had given up. We'd gone so far out of our way that my mother called Mrs Greaves to see if we'd gone to Midge's house instead. 'But now I have more stuff to do.'

'Don't lie,' Keith said 'Tell Mum the truth. You and the Midget are so slow, the only way you can get to school on time is if you leave before daylight.'

I ignored him. 'So I'm going now,' I said to my mother. 'Midge is waiting for me.' I started edging towards the door.

My mother came charging after me. 'Why are you dressed like that?' she wanted to know. She forgot nothing and she questioned everything. Mrs Vorha would have loved having my mother in her class. Mrs Vorha is big on the inquiring mind.

I was all innocent. 'Dressed like what?'

My mother put a hand on my shoulder. 'Dressed like that.' She pulled the glasses I was wearing away from my face so I had to look into her eyes. 'You don't usually wear a baseball cap and sun-glasses.'

The second part of our plan was disguise. Midge and I reckoned that if we dressed differently, those creeps wouldn't recognize us even if we did meet up with them.

The words 'baseball cap' and 'sun-glasses' caught my brother's attention. He put down the comic and looked over at me and started choking with laughter. 'Dig the android!' he howled. 'He thinks he's in an American movie!'

'Leave me alone!' I shouted back. 'Everybody wears baseball caps now.'

'Not everybody like you,' said my brother. 'Losers like you still wear bobble hats and anoraks.'

'Get off!' I ordered. If my mum wasn't still holding on to my glasses, I would have gone over and kicked him.

'That just better not be *my* baseball cap,' said my brother.

I stuck my tongue out at him. 'Don't worry, I wouldn't want to catch something from *you*. It's the one Uncle Bill brought me back from New York.'

My mother finally let go. 'Is this the new fad or something?' she asked. She looked sort of relieved. 'Is that what this is?'

She was a genius. 'That's it!' I was practically laughing myself. 'It's the new fad, Mum. It's really cool.'

'If you're into it, it's about as cool as molten lava,' said Keith.

This time it was my mother who ignored him. Mainly because she was still concentrating on me. 'What about breakfast?' she asked. 'You're not going to school on an empty stomach, are you?'

Breakfast! Here I was wondering if I was going to live through the morning, and my mother was worried about breakfast. If I didn't hurry, the only thing I was going to be having was a knuckle sandwich. I snatched the bread from her hand. 'I'll eat this on the way.'

My mother shouted something about after school, but I was moving too fast to really hear what she said. I was through the door before she realized there wasn't even any butter on the bread.

It was a good thing my mother didn't see Midge that morning or she would have been worried about a lot more than my breakfast. I only knew that the figure leaning against the tree was Midge because he was standing at the end of Midge's road and because he was short.

I waved, but he didn't wave back. Midge was wearing sun-glasses, too, but instead of a baseball cap he had on an old cloth hat and a denim jacket that was miles too big for him. The jacket and the hat both looked like they probably belonged to his dad.

'Is that you, Adam?' Midge asked as I came

up to him. He lifted the glasses. He's practically blind without his prescription lenses.

'No,' I said. 'It's Father Christmas.' Up close, he looked even weirder than he had from a distance. I punched him in the arm. 'You're supposed to be in disguise, Midge. Not in costume.'

He punched me back. It didn't hurt, though, because the jacket's sleeves were so long they covered his hands. 'It was either this or one of my mum's hats and my winter jacket.'

I didn't like to say, but if you asked me he wouldn't have looked any weirder in something pink with roses on it. I reckoned that it might not be so bad if we did run into those kids, they'd probably kill themselves laughing.

I suppose the good news was that we didn't run into *them*. The bad news was that we ran into Mr Altman instead. He was just locking his car when Midge and I came through the gates.

Midge said, 'Good morning, Sir.'

I said, 'Good morning, Sir.'

Mr Altman didn't speak at first. He just stared at us in silence, his eyes going from Midge to me and back again. I wished Midge had worn his own jacket. I wished he didn't have to look over his sun-glasses to see. And I really wished my Uncle Bill had brought me back one of those dark-blue baseball caps that said NY in white

letters, not a bright-green one that had Have a Nice Day written across the front in orange thread.

At last Mr Altman thought of something else to say. 'What's this?' he asked. 'Hallowe'en?'

'Stop worrying, will you?' I said. Midge was shuffling along beside me, looking at his watch. He'd got his proper glasses on now so he could see. 'It's Friday. They're not going to hang around for hours just to beat us up. I guarantee you, they'll be gone by now.'

Midge made a disbelieving face. It's funny, but even though he's adopted, he can look exactly like his mother. 'I still think we should've stayed at school a little longer.'

I sighed. 'Midge,' I said, 'if we'd stayed any longer the caretaker would've locked us in.' We slowed down as we reached the corner. 'And anyway, we're in disguise. Even if they are there, they're not going to recognize us, are they?'

'Um . . .' said Midge. He'd slowed down so much he was walking behind me.

We came to the corner. The street we usually walked down was empty except for a lady with one of those wicker basket on wheels and a couple of secondary-school girls, laughing like someone was tickling them.

'You see?' I turned back to Midge. 'I told you they wouldn't be there.'

Midge was still facing straight ahead. 'They *couldn't* be there,' he said.

I started to say that that was what I'd been trying to tell him all along, that they couldn't be there, but I didn't get any further than 'That's —'. There was something about the way he was staring past me and the funny way he said *they couldn't be* that made me look round. Coming towards us on the pavement were three boys on mountain bikes. I didn't even have to check the colours of the bikes. They were coming at us like guided missiles. This time Midge didn't ask me what to do.

He was half-way up the street before I knew what was happening.

'Dopey's mine!' the skinny one was shouting.

Dopey was me. I started to run.

My brother's a really good runner. He's tall and he's got these long legs and he knows how to breathe and all. I'm not a really good runner. I'm faster than Midge, but that's not saying a lot. I'd only gone a few metres when the boy with the really short hair cut me off.

'Where do you think you're going?' he sneered.

'Home,' I said. Which wasn't exactly true. He and his bike were blocking the pavement, and the two others were blocking me from behind, so I wasn't going anywhere, but I was still hopeful.

The three of them laughed.

Short hair got off his bike and let it crash to the ground. My mum would kill me if she saw me treating my bike like that.

'No you're not,' he informed me. He was smiling as he grabbed hold of my shirt with one hand. The other hand he made into a fist. 'You're going to give me your money, that's what you're going to do.'

'I can't,' I said. 'You already took it.'

He tightened his grip. 'Oh, poor little Dopey. You mean your mummy didn't give you any more?'

In my heart, I knew Mrs Greaves was right. It's better to stand up to things than to run away from them. Running away doesn't solve anything. And I knew Midge was right. My brother wouldn't run away. Only, Mrs Greaves and Keith weren't with us, and the teenagers from hell were. And neither Mrs Greaves nor Keith had some lunatic poking a fist as big as a pork roast in their face and I did.

'OK,' I said. I was already reaching into my pocket. 'OK, you can have my money.'

An ugly blond head peered over my shoulder. 'What else you got?' it asked. I was about to say that I didn't have anything except some old

gum wrappers, when two other voices started shouting at once.

The first voice was Midge's. 'Adam!' it was shouting. 'Adam! The bus!' It was true. A bus had stopped just ahead of us. Midge was standing next to it, holding on to the door.

The other voice belonged to some old lady who was beetling towards us, jabbing her umbrella in the air. 'You let go of that little boy!' she was shouting. 'Do you hear me? Let go of him right now!'

Short hair let go. First he hit me, and then he let go. It was a good thing I had my sun-glasses on or I might have got hurt. I didn't even stop long enough to scream in pain, I just ran for the bus.

'Get on the bus!' Midge was yelling. 'Quick, get on the bus!'

Like he had to tell me twice. It didn't even matter that the bus wasn't going our way. I didn't care if this bus was going to Iceland as long as we were on it. I pulled all my change out of my pocket as we jumped on and slapped it down on the tray.

'No pennies!' growled the driver.

The old lady was still screaming, but I could hear them coming up behind us as I tried to find some coins that weren't pennies.

'Hey, Dopey! Where do you think you and

Sleepy are going?' one of the boys was shouting. The other two were impersonating chickens.

Midge and I grabbed our tickets. We didn't look round.

'Don't think you can get away from us that easy! You two dwarfs are going to be sorry.'

Going to be sorry? I followed Midge down the aisle as the doors finally closed.

I collapsed on to the seat next to Midge. I sighed with relief. 'Boy, that was close.'

Midge was looking out the window. 'It's still close,' he said. 'They're right beside us.'

I looked over his shoulder. It was true. They were still on the pavement but they were right beside us. Scattering pedestrians in every direction, the teenage mutant thugs were keeping up with the bus.

I leaned back and looked straight ahead. 'Then we'll just have to stay on till we lose them,' I said.

I suppose I must basically be a very optimistic person because for some reason I didn't really think that would take very long.

Chapter Six

*T*he bus went past the heath. Then it passed the Spanish restaurant where my dad took us for my mum's birthday. Then it turned up the hill and past the cinema Midge and I sometimes go to on a Saturday. At the top of the hill there's this old church where a man with tattoos all over his face and about a dozen dogs lives. We passed that too.

Midge was squirming in his seat. 'My mother would kill me if she knew where we were,' he muttered. 'I'm not allowed to come this far on my own without permission.'

I kicked him. 'And I am?'

Instead of kicking me back, he glanced out the window. 'They're still there, Adam,' Midge informed me. 'What are we going to do? They're still there.'

The bus turned left. I kept my eyes straight ahead as the pizza restaurant, the video shop and the building where Midge's mother has her office went by. I didn't know what we were going to do, but I did know what we weren't going to do. We weren't going to get off the bus until those boys had turned back.

'Ignore them,' I told him. 'Don't let them see you looking at them. They've got to give up eventually.'

Midge was silent for a few minutes, sulking. 'What if they don't?' he finally asked. 'What if they don't give up?'

This wasn't something I really wanted to think about. My brother never gave up. He might have to wait days to get even with me for something, but it didn't matter. He'd wait years if he had to. Sometimes he had to wait so long that neither of us could remember what it was he was getting even for. What if these creeps were like Keith?

'Then we'll have to live on this bus for the rest of our lives,' I said. 'It's a good thing it goes by your mother's office, at least she'll be able to throw a packet of sandwiches in the window every lunch-time.'

'It's not funny,' said Midge. He lowered his voice. 'What if they're not real kids, Adam?' He was looking at my knee. 'Have you thought of that? What if they're evil spirits who have taken over the bodies of real kids and they never get tired or anything like that and we really do spend the rest of our lives on this bus?'

'Are you mad?' I stared back at him. How come everybody thought I was the one with the wild imagination? 'You've been watching too many horror videos, Midge. You –'

'Adam!' Midge cried. 'Adam, they're gone!'

'Are you sure?'

'Yeah,' he said. 'I'm sure.'

I pushed the bell.

'You do know what this means, don't you?' Midge asked as we climbed off. He didn't wait for me to answer. 'This means we'll never get rid of them now.'

We crossed the street to the return bus stop. I searched through my pockets but all I came up with was two pennies and some wrappers. 'No,' I said. 'What this means is that you'd better have the bus fare home because I'm completely skint.'

Midge didn't exactly answer. Midge just whimpered.

My mother was standing in the doorway as I came up the path. She started shouting the second she saw me. 'Adam Wiggins!' she was shouting. 'Where have you been? I sent your brother out looking for you.'

'What'd you do that for?' That was all I

needed. Didn't I have enough problems? Now Keith would never let me forget that my mother made him go look for me like I was a lost dog or something. The only comfort I had was that he hadn't been around when that old lady rescued me and Midge. He would have killed himself over that one.

'I'll tell you what I did it for,' yelled my mother. 'I did it because I was worried. It's gone five.'

What with all the strain I was under and having to walk home from miles away, I was pretty exhausted, but I acted cool and normal, like it wasn't any big deal. 'You didn't need to worry,' I said. 'It's Friday.' I strolled past her. 'I was with Midge.'

My mum was right behind me. 'But you weren't supposed to be with Midge, Adam. You were supposed to be with Mr Morris. I couldn't believe it when his receptionist called to see why you never turned up.'

I stopped in the middle of the hallway. I turned round. 'Mr Morris?' Mr Morris is my dentist.

She folded her arms in front of her. She sighed. My mother has this way of sighing that's more like a scream. My brother and I are the only ones who can make her sigh like that.

'What did I tell you when you were rushing

out of here this morning?' she demanded. 'Didn't I remind you about your appointment?'

So that was what she'd shouted after me. I couldn't decide whether she'd be madder if she knew I hadn't heard her or if she thought that I had. 'I suppose I forgot,' I said at last.

'You forgot.' It wasn't a question, but it wasn't exactly a statement either. It was more like she was taking notes. 'You've been acting very oddly the last few days,' said my mother. 'You come and go at odd times, you come home covered in scratches or with your trousers ripped and your bike broken –'

'I told you,' I said. 'It was an accident. Me and Midge crashed in the rain.'

'I know what you told me,' my mother answered. 'But I'd still like to know what's going on.'

I couldn't tell her the truth. I know my mother pretty well. If I told her these bigger boys were bullying me and I was afraid of them, she'd make a big stink about it. She'd find out who they were. She'd go up to the school and talk to their tutors and the headmistress, and then she'd talk to their parents. She's like that, my mum. She'd probably make me go with her to the school. She'd make the teenage terrorists apologize to me in front of everybody. She'd make them promise never to bother me or Midge again. Just the thought of it made me want to crawl into a hole. Not only would I be totally humiliated in front of the whole world, but it wouldn't make any difference. They wouldn't stop bothering me and Midge after that. They'd bother us more. They'd hound us. They'd torture us. They'd use us for loo paper. But even worse, once the whole world knew what weaklings me and Midge were, other kids would start bullying us. We'd never get away from them unless we moved to France. Or maybe Venezuela.

'Nothing's going on,' I said. I crossed my fingers and looked my mother in her X-ray eyes. 'Nothing at all.'

'You're sure?' asked my mother. 'You wouldn't lie to me?'

'No,' I said. I wouldn't lie, but I would stretch the truth.

'So where were you and the Midget?' asked Keith.

He was sitting on his bed, getting undressed, but I was already under the blankets. I didn't want to tell Keith where I'd been any more than I wanted to tell my mother. Especially since if I did tell him, after he stopped laughing he'd probably go straight to my mum. I pretended to be asleep.

Keith threw his socks at me. They smelled like a bunged-up sewer.

I sat up, choking. 'What are you trying to do, kill me?' I screamed.

My brother started laughing. 'I knew you were awake,' he said. 'You can't fool me.'

'I don't want to fool you.' I hurled the socks back at him but instead of landing in his face, they landed in the middle of the floor. 'I want you to leave me alone.'

This time he threw one of his trainers at me. It bounced off the wall and just missed Elvis. Elvis yelped and jumped off the bed.

'Is that the thanks I get?' asked Keith. 'Charlie and me gave up swimming to go looking for you and the Munchkin, you ungrateful cretin. The least you can do is tell me where you were.'

'I wasn't anywhere.' I turned my back on him. 'Me and Midge went to the heath.'

'Without the mutt?'

Most of the time it's hard to imagine how anyone as nice as my mum could have given birth to Keith. I mean, my mother's a regular human being, but my brother's more like something that crawled out of a cave. A dark underground cave filled with bats and dinosaur bones. Every once in a while, though, he reminds me of my mum. Like right then. Keith would have made nearly as good a detective as Caroline Wiggins.

'We didn't have time to collect him,' I said. 'We were in a hurry.'

'Don't lie. We checked the heath. You weren't there.'

'You couldn't check the whole heath,' I answered. 'You must've missed us.'

I heard the springs of his bed creak, and then the next thing I knew Keith was sitting on top of me.

'Get off!' I screamed. He weighs about a ton.

My brother threw a pillow over my head. 'Tell me,' he ordered. 'Tell me where you were. What dumb thing are you and the Munchkin up to this time?'

'I wasn't anywhere,' I mumbled. It's hard to breathe and talk at the same time when someone's sitting on you and you're being suffocated. I tried to throw him off but I couldn't move. 'I told you, we went to the heath.'

'I mean it, turd breath,' said Keith. He started bouncing up and down on me. 'You tell me or you're going to be sorry.'

Boy, did I wish I was an only child. At least Midge only got bullied when he left the house. Me, I didn't even have to leave home. I didn't even have to leave my room.

Chapter Seven

Midge and I spent Saturday at his house, playing on his Gameboy. We played most of the morning and all afternoon, but neither of us could beat my brother's record. Every hour or so, Midge's father would poke his head into the room and ask us if we weren't going to go outside. You'd think it was the first sunny day we'd ever had, the way he carried on.

'It's a beautiful day,' he kept saying. 'Why don't you boys go out and get some fresh air? You don't want to spend the weekend cooped up in a room.'

We told him that we did want to spend the weekend cooped up in a room, but we didn't tell him why. We just said that we were having a good time.

Midge's father said that when he was a boy he was outdoors playing ball or riding his bike no matter what the weather was like. When he was

a boy he couldn't stand to be indoors. He craved physical activity and adventure.

'Not us,' I said with more feeling than I'd intended. 'Physical activity and adventure are the last things we want.'

Midge's father shook his head sadly. He said he knew they should never have let Midge's grandparents buy him the Nintendo. He said he knew it would destroy Jerome's creativity and make him indolent. I didn't know what indolent meant, but I knew better than to ask. Once Midge's father got started it was hard to get him to stop. He banged on for over two hours one time because we made the mistake of asking him some simple question about whales.

Midge and I spent Sunday at my house, playing on my Gameboy. We played from the minute Keith left to meet Charlie till it was time for Midge to go home, but still neither of us even came close to beating my brother's record. Whenever she remembered we were there, my mother would stick her head into the room and ask us if we were planning to spend the entire day glued to a game. We said that we were.

'What about Elvis?' she wanted to know. 'He looks forward to spending Sunday outdoors.'

I patted Elvis's head. He didn't wake up, but he flicked his ear. 'Elvis is tired,' I told her. 'He wants to take it easy this weekend.'

'Elvis takes it easy all week long,' said my mother. 'He could use a little exercise.' She looked from Elvis to me and Midge. 'And so could you two.' She shook her head. 'You're certainly nothing like your brother,' said my mum. 'I can never keep him indoors.'

'Why would you want to?' I asked.

Monday morning we got a lift to school with Midge's mother because it was raining so hard that she felt sorry for us. After school we walked home with a bunch of kids and went straight to Midge's. I reckoned the teenagers from hell wouldn't spot us under our umbrella, but I didn't want to put my theory to the test. I suppose even they weren't dumb enough to hang around waiting for us in a monsoon.

'You see,' I said as I followed Midge through his front door, it's working out all right after all.'

In spite of everything, I was in a pretty good mood. Mrs Vorha was back from her conference. She said it was very interesting. It didn't sound very interesting, it sounded like a bunch of teachers sitting around talking about teaching, but Mrs Vorha said she learned a lot. She said the other teachers had been impressed with what we were doing in our class. I was really glad to see Mrs Vorha, and besides that, I was really glad that Midge and I had made it safely through another day.

Midge, however, wasn't in as good a mood as I was.

He hung up his jacket in the hall. 'Everything is not working out all right after all,' said Midge. His eyes darted towards the living-room door. We could hear his mother talking on the telephone inside.

'Yes it is. We just have to take things one day at a time.' I hung my jacket beside Midge's.

'I don't want to take things one day at a time,' Midge informed me. 'I can't take much more of this, Adam. I'm tired of sneaking around like a criminal.'

'Don't think of us as criminals,' I said. 'Think of us as spies.' Spies sounded a lot more fun than criminals.

But not to Midge.

'I don't want to think of us as anything but little boys,' said Midge. We could hear his mum saying good-bye. He lowered his voice. 'And I'd like to see us live to be big boys.' He lowered his voice even more. 'I mean it, Adam, I'm tired of living in fear.'

'And I'm not?' I was the one who'd had almost a whole week's pocket money stolen. I was the one whose front wheel was bent. I was the one who'd been punched in his sun-glasses.

After all I'd gone through, this was the thanks I got. 'I'm the one who lies awake half the night, trying to come up with ways of surviving,' I told Midge's back as he led the way down the hall.

'Well, you don't have to,' said Midge. He shut the kitchen door behind us. 'I know how we can solve this problem in about ten minutes.'

'Oh, yeah?' I said. 'And what's that? Give them our lunch money every morning? Let them have anything they want from us?'

'No,' said Midge. 'Tell Keith.'

'Tell Keith?'

I couldn't have heard him right. I was sure I must have water in my ears from walking home in the rain. But I was wrong.

Midge nodded. 'It would solve everything.'

'Tell Keith?' He thought this was a solution?

He shoved me out of the way and opened the fridge. 'Yes,' said Midge. 'Tell Keith. What's so hard about that?'

'You want me to tell Keith that we're being bullied?'

Midge put a container of juice on the worktop. 'Yes, Adam. That's what I want you to do.'

'And do you know what he'll do if I tell him that?' I stepped back as Midge heaved himself up on the worktop so he could reach the cupboard. 'Huh, Midge? Do you know what he'll do?'

Midge handed me two glasses. 'Keith will take care of those boys for us, that's what he'll do, Adam.' He handed me the biscuit tin. 'He'll make them leave us alone.'

'No he won't,' I said. 'He'll laugh himself sick, that's what he'll do. He'll think it's the funniest thing he's ever heard. He'll torment me with it for the rest of my life.'

Midge squidged up his mouth. 'If I had a big brother, I'd tell him.'

'If you had a big brother he wouldn't be Keith,' I pointed out. I'd rather tell my mother than tell my brother. My mother might embarrass and humiliate me in front of the entire universe, but she wouldn't laugh at me. 'There'll be Martians in Buckingham Palace before I tell Keith. There'll be buffaloes in Hyde Park.'

'They'll be visiting us both in hospital if you don't tell him,' said Midge.

'That's not true.' I watched Midge pour out two glasses of juice. 'I don't need Keith's help. I can fight my own battles.'

Midge gave me a look. It was not a look of total confidence. 'No you can't,' he assured me. 'If you try to take on those boys they'll knock you out cold before you even make a fist.'

I picked up my drink. 'Thanks for having so much faith in me,' I said sourly.

'Faith has nothing to do with it,' said Midge. 'I'm just being realistic. We can't spend the rest of the year trying to stay out of their way. It's not only stupid, it's impossible.' He bit into a custard cream. 'And we can't hide in our rooms every weekend, Adam. Our parents are going to force us out sooner or later.'

I helped myself to a biscuit. 'I know that,' I said. 'I'm not planning to hide from them for ever, Midge. I've decided that your mother's right. I'm going to stand up to them.'

'Oh sure you are,' shrieked Midge. Soggy biscuit crumbs sprayed all over the worktop. 'What are you going to stand on, Adam, an armoured tank?'

'Oh ha ha ha,' I said. 'Very funny, I don't think.' I took another biscuit. 'For your information, what I'm going to do is I'm going to learn karate.'

I'd seen it in a film. There was this skinny little kid who moved to a new city and these big boys with bad attitudes started picking on him. No matter where he went or what he did, they'd show up and they'd punch him. He was afraid to leave the house. Just like me and Midge. He got a black eye and I had a pair of broken sunglasses and torn trousers. His bike got messed up and so did mine. And then he met this old bloke from one of those Eastern countries where they know all about self-defence, and the old bloke offered to teach the skinny kid karate. The old bloke made him catch flies with chopsticks and stand on the front of a rowing-boat and stuff like that, but in the end the kid became this big karate expert, beat the bullies, and won the championship and all.

I reckoned if it worked for him, it could work for me.

Midge didn't.

'This isn't going to work, Adam,' Midge whispered. He was whispering because we were in the library near our school. 'Life isn't like films, you know. You can't change just like that.'

The reason we were in the library was because I needed a book. The only person I knew who came from an Eastern country was Mrs Lim. Even if she was speaking to me (which she still wasn't), I was pretty sure she didn't know much about karate. Gardening was more Mrs. Lim's thing. I wasn't discouraged, though. I thought I could pick up the basics from a book, and then I could practise on Midge.

'Yes you can,' I whispered back. I pointed to the shelf of books in front of us: *Teach Yourself Tennis*, *Weight-lifting at Home*, *Learn to Ski in a Weekend* ... The number of things you could learn from books was endless. I wondered if they

had one on being a human being that I could get for Keith.

'This is it.' I pulled a thin black book from the shelf and read the title out to Midge. '*Karate: Its Theory and Practice.*'

He looked over my shoulder while I started flipping through the pages. There was a long introduction by the author, who was a famous martial-arts expert. He didn't come from Okinawa, though. His name was Alan Draper and he came from Manchester. There was a chapter on the history of karate and there was one on what you were supposed to wear. Then there was Course One, the Beginner's Course. That was for me. It had exercises to get your mind ready. It had exercises to get your body ready. It had step-by-step illustrations of men in short jackets and loose trousers flipping around other men in short jackets and loose trousers. It had diagrams that showed you where to stand, and how to step, and how to move your body. It even had photographs. I grinned at Midge. It didn't look hard at all.

Chapter Eight

I walked home slowly from the library, looking at the pictures in the karate book on the way. I was so excited that for the first time in days I didn't worry about running into the teenagers from hell. I just strolled along like a normal person who isn't expecting to turn a corner and get beaten up. I imagined that I'd already mastered the lessons in the book. I could see myself dressed in that white jacket and those baggy trousers, punching and kicking and shouting out like the blokes in the pictures.

I kicked open our front gate. 'Uh!' I yelled. I punched the air.

'Have a good day at school, Adam?'

My mum was behind the hedge, scraping paint off some old table she got in a junk shop. She didn't half scare me, but I managed not to scream.

I was glad I'd already put the book in my satchel so I didn't have to explain that. I smiled

so she wouldn't think I was acting weird or anything. 'It was all right.'

She was giving me one of her Detective Inspector Caroline Wiggins looks. 'What did you do today, then?' she asked.

'Do?' I knew we must have done something, but my head was so full of *Karate: Its Theory and Practice* that at first I couldn't remember what.

'Yes,' said my mother. 'What did you do?'

It came back to me. 'Oh, I know! Mrs Vorha says that my essay I wrote on being in a wheel-chair has been short-listed in the competition. She says they'll be announcing the winner soon.'

'Short-listed!' My mother stopped looking like she thought I was a suspect. 'Why, Adam, that's wonderful! Wait till your father hears!'

I hadn't thought much about it when Mrs Vorha told me the news at the end of class because I was trying to figure out the safest route to the library, but now that I saw my mum's reaction, I was feeling pretty pleased.

My mum dusted paint flakes from her hands and came over and gave me a big hug. 'I must say, your father and I certainly have a lot to be proud of,' she said. 'Keith was chosen for the British junior team today and your essay's been short-listed in a competition.'

'Keith was chosen for the British junior team? The one that's going to play in Europe?'

'Isn't that terrific?'

My mum was still smiling, but I wasn't. Somehow, getting my essay short-listed in some dumb biscuit competition didn't seem like much next to making the British junior team.

There was some really good news, though. Keith was spending the night at Charlie's. I couldn't believe I could be that lucky. The only time I had our room to myself was when Keith spent the night at Charlie's. And the only time I could do anything really private was when I had our room to myself. I couldn't cut my toe-nails when Keith was around without him making a major deal out of it, forget anything else. So I took it as a sign – a good sign.

I called Midge to tell him. 'You see,' I said. 'I knew I was doing the right thing. My luck is changing at last.'

'It couldn't get much worse,' said Midge.

Right after tea, I told my parents I had a lot of homework to do and Elvis and I went to my room. I locked the door. I didn't lock the door because I was afraid someone would just walk in and want to know what I was doing, but because I could lock the door. The one time I locked the door when Keith was around and bothering me, he unscrewed the whole knob and my dad got mad at me. I took the karate book out from under my mattress where I'd hidden it and I stretched out on my bed.

The first thing I read was the karate oath. It was something like the Boy Scout pledge. It was pretty cool. *I have no weapons*, it said, *but should I be forced to defend myself, my principles or my honour, then here are my weapons – 'karate' – my empty hands.*

I went on to the introduction. Alan Draper and I had a lot in common. Alan Draper decided to learn martial arts when he was thirteen and some kids at school kept beating him up. I liked him right away. He said he tried several sorts of self-defence, but that he liked karate best. I hadn't realized how many forms of self-defence there were, or how hard most of their names were to pronounce. Elvis was snoring by the time I got through the list. Alan Draper claimed that the co-ordination karate developed in you would make it possible for three opponents to receive a blow at precisely the same moment. That sounded like just what I wanted. I couldn't wait to see the faces of the teenage terrorists when they each received a blow from me at exactly the same moment.

Alan Draper went on to talk about how much enjoyment karate had given him in the years he'd been studying it. There was a picture of him and he looked pretty old, so I reckoned he'd been studying it for a long time. This worried me a little. I didn't want to spend years learning karate. I didn't have years. I had to have it mastered by the end of the week at the latest.

The next section told a bit about the history and philosophy of karate. I thought the idea was to be able to beat up somebody else even if he was bigger than you were, but the book said that the spirit of karate was passive, not aggressive. It said karate was about form and balance. It said karate wasn't about violence, but about non-violence. This was news to me. The teenagers from hell weren't interested in form and balance, and they definitely liked violence a lot. I skipped some of that section and went to the first picture where someone was flicking someone else through the air.

The one thing I'd been right about was that size didn't matter. You didn't have to be tall and built like an armoured tank. You didn't have to have muscles or be able to run like a panther. All you had to know was when to pull back, when to push forward, where to grab your opponent and how to slip out of his way. The book said that the beauty of karate was that it was as simple and natural as breathing, and just as effective.

I must have fallen asleep around the part where Alan Draper was talking about how natural karate was.

Midge and I were walking home from school. It was winter and the sky was grey. Instead of our usual route, we were walking through this big deserted field. The only things in the field beside us were these gigantic black birds, strutting around and stretching their wings. All of a sudden it started getting really dark. Midge and I didn't say anything to each other, but we both knew that something was going to happen. Something bad. We walked faster. The field disappeared. We were on a narrow, dirty street of old, empty buildings with broken windows and crumbling walls. There was rubbish all over the ground. Things were creaking and banging in the wind. Someone started laughing. A nasty laugh. When the laughing got softer, we heard something else. We heard someone crying for help.

Midge turned to me, a look of fear and horror on his face. I put my finger to my lips. I knew that he'd recognized that voice, too. It was my brother, Keith.

I motioned Midge to stay where he was and I crept silently to the end of the street. Standing flat against a wall, I peered round the corner. Three boys were standing in a circle in the middle of the road. One of the boys was tall and thin and his hair was so short you couldn't tell what colour it was. One of the boys was tall and chubby and had almost black hair and really light-blue eyes. The one who was laughing was the biggest. He wasn't just tall, he was broad and solid. He looked like he was going to be Arnold Schwarzenegger when he grew up. In the middle of the circle was Keith. He was down on the ground and he was begging for mercy. The thin boy and the chubby boy were kicking him.

'Don't hurt him too much,' ordered the boy who was laughing. 'Save something for me.' Then he laughed even more.

I stepped out of the shadows. 'No,' I said. 'Save something for me.'

The three of them turned in my direction.

'Adam!' gasped Keith. 'Adam, get away from here. Save yourself!'

'Yeah, Adam,' said the laugher. 'Run away like a chicken. Go home and cry to your mummy.'

Very, very slowly, I started walking towards them. 'I'm not going anywhere,' I said. 'And the one who's going to be crying isn't me, it's you.'

This made them all crack up.

The two who were kicking Keith stopped. 'You!' they jeered. 'What are you going to do? Bore us to tears?'

I was almost up to them by then. They were facing me in a line.

Keith was sobbing. 'Adam,' he begged me. 'Adam, please, forget about me. Just tell Mum I love her and save yourself.'

'You're my brother,' I said. 'I'm not leaving here without you.'

The big boy spat on the ground. 'You don't scare us,' he said. 'You're nothing but a wimp. Lucinda Moon once knocked you down. You don't have any muscles. You can't swim or play football. You can't control your own dog. You run like a girl.'

I smiled, slowly. 'There's one other thing about me you should know.'

'Oh, yeah?' The three of them sneered. 'And what's that?'

This time I laughed. 'I have a triple black belt in karate.'

I was still laughing when the last one crumbled to the ground. I tied them up with some rope that was lying around. They were crying like babies and kicking the pavement. I helped Keith to his feet.

'How can I ever thank you?' he whispered. His voice was choked with emotion. 'You saved my life.'

The sound of kicking got louder.

'You don't have to thank me,' I said. 'It was nothing. It wasn't a big deal.'

'But you're a hero,' said my brother. 'You're

going to get a medal. You're going to have your picture in the paper.'

All of a sudden Elvis and my mother were beside us. Elvis was licking my face. My mum was shouting. 'Adam! Adam, you're so brave and strong! No wonder I always liked you better than Keith.'

I opened my eyes. Elvis really was licking my face. And my mother really was shouting. Only she wasn't telling me how brave and strong I was and how she always liked me better than my brother. She was trying to get in.

'Adam Wiggins,' she was shouting. 'Adam Wiggins, you open this door.'

Chapter Nine

I thought I'd be able to start kicking and punching right away, but Alan Draper had a whole bunch of things he said I had to do first. Like prepare my mind. I wasn't sure what he meant by that, so I sat with my eyes closed for a few minutes, trying to think about nothing. The next thing I was supposed to do was practise breathing, but I reckoned that I could skip that because I'd been breathing for eight years already without any trouble. Then came the more exciting part, preparing my body. According to Alan Draper, you didn't have to be big and muscular, but you did have to be in shape.

I was lying on my stomach on the floor. '*Finger* push-ups?' I asked. 'Are you sure that's what it says? *Finger* push-ups?'

'That's what it says,' said Midge. He was sitting on his bed, reading the karate book to me. He held it up so I could see the illustration.

The figure at the top of the page was definitely pushing himself up by his fingertips.

'How many times do I have to do that?'

Midge frowned at the page. 'Fifteen.'

I got my fingertips into position, but I couldn't lift my body even a little. 'What comes after that?' I asked.

'Push-ups on your first two knuckles,' said Midge.

'Get off!'

Midge waved the book at me. 'It's true, Adam. After finger push-ups comes knuckle push-ups.'

I didn't fancy pushing myself by my knuckles any more than by my fingertips. And I reckoned I had about as much chance of being able to do it, too. Which was no chance at all. 'What's after that?'

Midge squinted at the tiny print. 'Push-aways.'

That didn't sound too difficult. Living with my brother, I was used to being pushed away. 'What do I do?'

Midge read out what I had to do. 'Face the wall, and make your body straight from head to heels.'

I stood up and faced the wall. I made my body as straight as I could.

'Your weight should be on your hands and feet,' read Midge.

'Right,' I answered. This was easy.

Midge looked from the page to me. 'No, Adam. Your hands should be at eye-level and your feet half a metre from the wall.'

I corrected myself. 'Go on.'

He cleared his throat. 'OK,' said Midge. 'Now, keeping your body and arms straight, push yourself away from the wall until your weight is on your fingertips.'

Alan Draper had a thing about fingertips. I pushed. My fingers slipped and I hit the wall.

'Give me that!' I picked myself up and grabbed the book from Midge's hands. I turned the page. 'Here,' I cried triumphantly. 'I knew there had to be something better. What about "arm resistance" or "shoulder rotations"?'

Midge was shaking his head. 'I think you need something a little more drastic. Let's face it, Adam, you're not just trying to strengthen your muscles, you're trying to get some.' He leaned over my shoulder. 'What about using my mother's weights? Then you could do the "two-hand curl". That looks like it would work.'

Mrs Greaves isn't short, but she's skinny. Whenever I stay for tea or whatever, she always has to get Mr Greaves to open the pickle jars and stuff like that. It wasn't going to be like using Frank Bruno's weights, was it? I reckoned I'd be safe enough with them.

'Are you sure your mother uses these weights?' I grunted. They were a lot heavier than they looked.

Midge was studying the instructions for the 'two-hand curl'. 'Of course I'm sure. My father doesn't do weight-lifting. He has a bad back.' He looked up at me. 'You're holding it wrong,' Midge informed me. 'You have to have your palms facing the ground and the bar against your chest.'

I turned my palms so that they were facing the ground. I pulled the bar against my chest.

'Now raise the bar over your head and bring it behind your neck,' said Midge.

I took this in. 'Behind my neck? Are you sure?'

Midge sighed. 'Adam,' he said, 'if you don't trust me to read the directions, then read them yourself. Bring the bar behind your neck. That's what it says.'

This time when I fell over, I brought down the shelf with Midge's collection of glass animals on it.

My mother was next door fixing Mrs Pitellis' electric kettle and my brother was at football practice, so Midge and I had the house to ourselves for a little while.

'We'll start with the very first escape defence,'

I said. 'It's called "Resisting a Left-hand Grab from the Front".' The skinny terrorist was always grabbing me by my jacket, so this was perfect.

'Why can't I be the one who's escaping?' asked Midge. 'How come I have to be the bad guy?'

'Because I'm the one who's learning karate,' I explained for about the fourth time that afternoon. 'You're just my partner.'

I put the glass bowl my mum keeps on the coffee-table on the book to hold the page open.

'But I don't want to be your partner,' said Midge. 'I still think the whole thing's a dumb idea. I still think we should tell your brother.'

I decided to do to Midge what my mother does to me when I try to argue her out of something. I ignored him.

'All right,' I said. 'Now here's what you do. You grab my shirt with your left hand.'

Midge looked at me doubtfully. 'And then what happens?'

I looked down at the book. 'Then I step back on my left foot and grab your hand with my left hand while I hit your elbow with my right arm.' I decided to skip the part that said 'CAUTION – this can cause a sprain or fracture'.

Midge was still looking distrustful. 'That's it?'

I read on. 'Unless that doesn't work. Then I have to use the "five-finger thrust to the eyes".'

'I don't fancy the sound of that,' said Midge. He stood on tiptoes and peered over my shoulder. 'What's that?' he squeaked. 'It says "TO BE USED ONLY IN AN EXTREME EMERGENCY".'

I shoved him away. 'Don't get your knickers in a twist. I'm not really going to hit you. Alan Draper says always to stop before you make contact. It's just to teach my body what to do.'

'What if you hit me by accident? What if you poke out my eyes?'

'Through your glasses?' He could be a right niggler when he wanted. 'I'm not going to hit you, all right? We're just going through the motions.' I stood in front of him like the man in the book. 'Now, grab my shirt with your left hand.'

'You swear you're not going to touch me?'

'Midge!'

He grabbed my shirt. I stepped back on my left foot. I grabbed his left hand. But before I could whack his elbow with my right arm, something large and dark came charging at us from across the room, barking like a lunatic.

My mother came in just as Midge, Elvis, the coffee-table and I crashed to the floor.

'Will it do me any good to ask what you two were doing?' asked my mother.

*

Alan Draper said that if you practised the basic strikes every day, you'd make rapid progress. The only time I could practise the basic strikes was when I was in the bathroom. So that week I took a bath every night. A long bath.

I practised while the bath was filling. I practised some more while the water got cold. I put in some more hot water and practised while that was running. I took a really quick bath, got out of it, got into my pyjamas, and practised a while longer. I even practised while the water was draining from the bath.

By Thursday night, though, my brother was getting suspicious.

Keith was lying on his bed, reading a comic, when I came into the room in my pyjamas and dressing-gown. He watched me put my jeans and shirt on my chair. Then he threw an apple core at me.

'What's going on?' he wanted to know. 'Don't tell me the littlest android's got a girl-friend.'

I sat down at my desk to finish my homework, my back to Keith. 'I don't know what you're talking about,' I said. Which was true. I had no idea what he was going on about now.

My brother explained. 'You go to school early, you come home late, and you spend half the night in the bathroom. Me and Charlie reckon you must have a crush on someone.'

'It took two of you to come up with such a dumb idea?' I said. I was pretty relieved that he was so far from the truth. 'You're both mad.' Keith always knows when I am lying.

Like now.

'Are we?' he asked. 'Then what were you doing in Mansfield Street yesterday afternoon?'

I couldn't help it, I looked round. 'How do you know that?' I blurted out.

Keith smiled, well pleased with himself. 'Me and Charlie were coming back from the bike shop and we saw you and the Midget walking out of Mansfield.' Actually, it wasn't a smile, it was a sneer. 'What were you doing, Adam? Unless you've changed schools, Mansfield's miles out of your way.'

I turned back to my notebook. 'We were taking a walk, that's all. It's a free country, isn't it? We can take a walk if we want.'

'Course you can,' said Keith. 'And is that why you take a bath every night? Because it's a free country?'

Usually I only think of good answers to my brother afterwards. You know, after he's asleep or the next day or something. But this time one came to me right away. 'No,' I said. 'I take a bath every night because I don't want to stink like you.'

My brother doesn't have my problem. He

always knows what to say. 'Don't worry about it,' said my brother. 'You stink just like yourself.' A peanut shell hit the back of my head and landed on the desk. 'So why do you go to school so early now? Are you trying to become the caretaker, Adam? Is that it?'

I was staring at the page of sums I'd copied out, but they were just a bunch of numbers. They didn't make any sense. Why did we go to school so early?

Another peanut shell hit me in the neck. 'Well, Adam? You and the Midget can't have something to do before class every single day.' He snorted. He sounded exactly like the pig we saw at the city farm. 'Unless you're walking by somebody's *house* . . .'

'We're not walking by anybody's house, we just go early, that's all.'

'You two mini-cretins don't do anything for no reason,' said my brother. 'And I'm going to find out what it is.' He snorted again. 'Or should I say *who*?'

Chapter Ten

My brother flicked a soggy cornflake at me. 'How come you're not rushing off to school?' he asked. He made his voice go funny. 'Isn't your girl-friend around today?'

My mum didn't say anything, but she stopped sipping her coffee and looked at me.

I would have kicked Keith under the table but I couldn't reach him and I was afraid of hitting my mum instead. It always makes her mad. Keith had teased me all night long about having a girl-friend. Even after we turned out the lights he made up this song about nerds in love. I tried to suffocate him with my pillow, but he threw me off and I knocked the golden retriever lamp my grandad made us off the dresser. That's why I didn't want to make my mum mad. She already was mad. And that's why I wasn't going early. I was hoping he'd give up if I acted like everything was normal.

'I don't feel like going early today,' I said. I

scooped up my cereal so hard that milk sloshed out of the bowl. 'And for the ten millionth time, Keith, I don't have a girl-friend.'

But my brother never gives up. He smiled. 'Sure you don't, Adam,' he said in this sickly, sweet voice. 'I believe you.' He winked. 'Mum believes you, too, don't you, Mum?'

'Leave your brother alone, Keith,' ordered my mother.

'Me?'

'Yes, *you*,' said my mother, but she was still looking at me. My mother always likes to know what's going on. 'Does this mean you're going to be home to take Elvis for his walk at the old time this afternoon?' she wanted to know.

'Of course I am,' I answered. 'Where else would I be?'

'Walking past *her* house, hoping to catch a glimpse of *her*,' said my brother, practically choking with laughter. He just never gives up.

I didn't have a chance to tell Midge that I was going to be late, so I didn't expect to see him at the end of the road, but he was there. I didn't expect to see the teenagers from hell at the end of Midge's road either, but they were there too.

None of them saw me, they were too busy.

The teenagers from hell had Midge up against a brick wall. The fat one and the one who was practically bald were running around, taunting Midge and laughing. Son of the Terminator was holding out his hands while Midge dug into his pockets.

I didn't know what to do.

I mean, I knew what I should do. I should rescue Midge. But even though I'd been studying karate for nearly a week, I wasn't so sure I could take on all three of them. Not at such short notice. My mind hadn't been exercised. I wished I had Elvis with me. They were scared of him.

'I think he's going to cry,' the skinny one was shouting. 'Look, I think the dwarf's going to cry.'

The one taking Midge's money laughed. 'No he's not. He's going to wet himself.'

I thought about Elvis for a second. Noise. Alan Draper said that it helped throw your opponent off-guard if you shouted. He said it was like a bear growling. Or a dog barking, I reckoned. It gave you a psychological advantage.

The karate shout was the one thing I knew I was really good at. I decided to give it a go. Maybe if I surprised them and made enough noise, I could scare them. Midge's house was only a few doors down. All I had to do was scare them long enough for us to get there.

I took a deep breath. And then I started

running towards them, yelling and screaming as loud as I could. I didn't even look at Midge or stop or anything, I just ran right through them, howling like a dog, heading for Midge's house. Everybody ran after me. I prayed that the kid right behind me was Jerome Greaves and not somebody else. I ran up the path to Midge's front door.

'Ring the bell!' Midge shouted. 'Ring the bell!'

I rang the bell.

'Don't think this is the end of it!' Son of the Terminator was shouting. 'You think you're clever, Dopey, but you owe me. Just you wait.'

The door opened. Mrs Greaves looked surprised. 'Jerome!' she said. 'Adam! What are you two doing here?'

Midge shoved me past her. 'I forgot something,' he said.

Behind us I heard the skinny kid calling, 'See you later, Adam. We'll wait for you after school.'

'Yeah,' the fat one chimed in. 'Don't be late.'

After the roll call, Mrs Vorha said she had an announcement to make. 'This concerns Adam,' she added.

Everybody looked at me. Usually when everybody looks at me, I get embarrassed. But today I didn't care. There was a pretty good chance that I was going to be dead soon, what did it matter?

Mrs Vorha was looking at me, too. She was smiling. 'I have some very good news,' she said.

The only good news Mrs Vorha could give me was that she was leaving for Alpha Centuri in an hour and wanted me to go with her. I reckoned I'd be all right if the teenage mutant thugs grabbed me from the front with one hand, grabbed me from the front with two hands, grabbed me from the back with one hand, or grabbed me from my right side. Anything else, though, and I was in trouble. That was as far as I'd got in Alan Draper's book.

'Adam,' Mrs Vorha was saying, 'I'm very happy to be able to tell you that your wheelchair essay has been chosen as the best of its age-group by the judges of the competition.' I'd never seen her smile like that before. 'You won, Adam! Isn't that wonderful?'

Everybody clapped.

'Adam,' said Mrs Vorha, 'I thought you'd be pleased. You're going to be given a special certificate, and the local paper is going to reprint your essay. Your words will be in print. The first publication of many, I hope.'

'I am pleased,' I said. I forced myself to smile. 'I'm really pleased.' And I was. I liked writing, and I'd really enjoyed writing that essay. But all

I could think was that I'd be even more pleased if I was around to see my words in print.

They were waiting for us right outside the gates. When they saw me and Midge, the three of them carried on like we were their long-lost friends or something. They were smiling and laughing. In loud voices they said how good it was to see us and how they'd been afraid we weren't coming.

The mean one led the way.

The fat one started walking next to Midge.

The skinny one put an arm around my shoulder. 'Adam,' he said, 'wait till you see the spot we've picked out. You're going to love it.'

I didn't love it. It was up on the heath, in this little clearing in the woods.

'No one will bother us here,' said the leader. He laughed. 'We'll be able to have a nice, sensible talk in private.'

The skinny one patted my head. 'We're going to tell you two little geeks what you're going to do for us from now on.' He was patting my head really hard. 'Just so's we understand each other.'

'Get your hand off me,' I said. I reckoned that if we were going to fight I might as well start standing up to them now.

'Oooh,' said the chubby kid. 'Adam's got an attitude.'

The skinny kid put his face really close to mine.

'Who's going to make me?' he asked. 'You?'

The other two creeps considered this a major joke.

I stood up as tall as I could. They didn't notice, but I didn't care. Alan Draper said the basis of karate was confidence. If you were confident and thoughtful, if you didn't give in to fear and panic, you could overcome any opponent.

'Yes,' I said. 'I'm going to make you.'

They found this even funnier.

'Gosh,' said the mean one. 'I'm really scared.'

He reached out and grabbed me by my jacket. It was a right-hand lapel grab from the front. I wasn't sure about the right hand. Did that mean I stepped back on my right foot? The other thing was, he was holding me a lot tighter than Midge did when we practised. Choking me, in fact.

'I'm warning you,' I said. 'Let go of me, or you'll be sorry.'

This was the funniest joke yet.

'You heard my brother,' said a voice behind me. 'Let go of him or you're going to be really sorry.'

It was like someone had spoken the magic words or something. First, all three of them looked over Midge's and my head, and then the mutant thug let go.

'Wiggins,' said Son of the Terminator. He was smiling, but it wasn't the way he smiled at me. He was scared. 'Wiggins, is this your brother?'

Midge and I turned round. Keith and Charlie had dropped their bikes and were coming towards us. They were walking slowly, like they had all the time in the world. They looked really big. Bigger than the teenagers from hell. Talk about confidence. I wondered if Keith had ever read Alan Draper's book.

'Yeah,' said Keith. 'That's my brother.' He looked at me. 'You all right, Adam?'

I nodded. 'Yeah,' I said. 'I'm fine.'

Keith turned back to the mutant thugs. 'That's good,' he said. 'Because anybody stupid enough to hurt my brother has to deal with me.'

It was like being in a film.

The three teenagers from hell took a step backwards for every step my brother and Charlie took forwards.

'We didn't know he was your brother,' said the fat kid. 'You know we wouldn't hurt your brother.'

'Oh, sure,' said Keith. 'I know that.' He stopped beside me. 'Are these creeps the reason your bike got broken, Adam?' he asked. 'Is this why you've been acting so weird?'

I nodded again, but I couldn't quite speak. Half of me wanted to tell Keith to go away, that me and Midge could take care of ourselves. But the other half of me was really glad to see him. I don't think I'd ever been gladder to see anyone in my life. It was like having Superman as your brother.

'They mugged us,' Midge blurted out. 'And they've been waiting for us after school and chasing us all over.'

'Tough guys,' said Keith. 'Beating up little kids.'

'I told you,' said the biggest one. 'We didn't know he was your brother. We wouldn't have gone near him if we knew he was your brother.'

Keith put his hand on my shoulder. 'Why don't you and Midge take your bike and go home?' asked Keith. 'Me and Charlie want to have a little talk with your friends.'

'My bike? But my bike's broken.' I looked back to where he and Charlie had left their bikes. It was true. Keith had been riding my bike, not his.

'I fixed it,' said Keith. So that was why he stayed over at Charlie's the other night. That was why he'd been coming from the bike shop on Wednesday afternoon. 'I reckoned if I didn't fix yours you might borrow mine.'

'So what'd you do?' I asked when Keith got home. 'Did you beat them up?'

'No,' said Keith. 'I'm not going to risk hurting myself fighting with those jerks. Me and Charlie just talked to them, that's all.' He sat down beside me on my bed. 'You weren't really going to fight them, were you, Adam?'

'I didn't have much choice,' I answered. 'It was more like they were going to fight me.'

He was looking at me the way my mum looks at me sometimes. You know, stunned with disbelief. 'But weren't you afraid?'

I didn't see any reason for telling him the truth. I never admit any weakness to Keith if I can help it.

'Not really,' I said coolly. The funny thing was, once I said it I realized it was sort of true. Standing up to those boys hadn't been half as terrifying as imagining standing up to them had been. When I'd been talking back to them, being scared hadn't mattered. I knew they were going to beat me up, but I also knew I wasn't going to make it easy for them.

'I'd have been afraid,' said my brother. 'I would have fought them, too, but I still would have been afraid.'

The way he said 'I would have fought them, too' made it sound like we were the same sort of person. I stared at him. 'Go on! You're not afraid of anything.'

'Course I am,' said Keith. 'It's only natural. Everybody's afraid of something.'

'Well, I had a secret weapon,' I said. 'I've been practising karate.'

'Karate?' I could see he was trying not to smile.

I pulled Alan Draper's book out from under my pillow. 'See,' I said. 'I've been practising with Midge.'

He stopped trying not to smile. 'With the Munchkin? You've got to be joking.'

'No,' I said. 'I was just beginning to get the hang of it.'

He started flipping through the book. 'You know, I've always fancied karate myself,' said my brother. 'Maybe we could ask Dad if he'd let us have lessons. Then we could practise together.'

'But you'll be better at it than I am,' I said. I hadn't meant to say that, I'd meant to say that I thought that was a great idea, but somehow it slipped out.

Keith gave me another puzzled look. 'What makes you say that?' he asked.

What made me say that. Now who was joking?

'Because you're better at everything,' I said.

'No I'm not,' said my brother. 'You're as good as I am at school. You're better at drawing and writing and stuff like that. Didn't you just win that competition?' he asked. 'I couldn't write a prize-winning essay for anything.'

'You fixed my bike,' I answered. 'I couldn't do that.'

My brother gave me a shove. 'I bet you could if I showed you how.'

When my essay was printed in the paper my mother bought about twenty copies. She sent them to my aunts and uncles and to my grandparents and to all her friends. There was a photograph of me next to the essay and the bit that told about the competition and what the assignment had been. The caption underneath the picture said: *A future Shakespeare?* I put it up on my pin-board. Keith cut the picture out and stuck it in his wallet. 'What are you doing that for?' I asked him.

'It's for when I go to Europe with the team,' he said. 'So I can show everybody what my brother's like.'

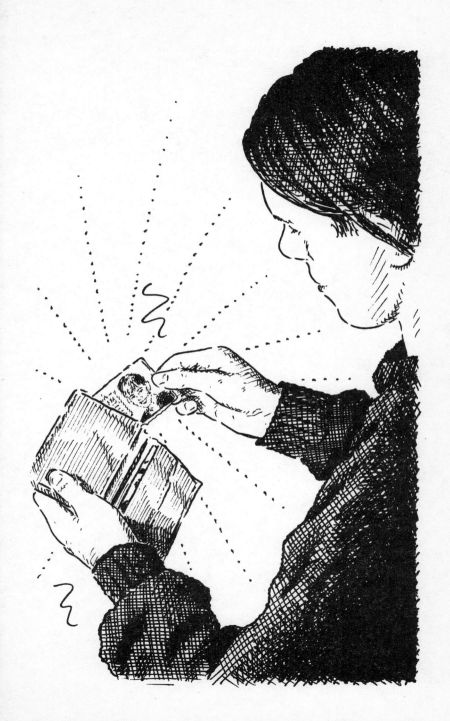